IGGY
THE LEGEND

LOOK FOR IGGY'S OTHER TRIUMPHS

The Best of Iggy

Iggy Is Better Than Ever

Iggy Is the Hero of Everything

IGGY
THE LEGEND

ANNIE BARROWS

ILLUSTRATED BY SAM RICKS

putnam

G. P. Putnam's Sons

G. P. PUTNAM'S SONS
An imprint of Penguin Random House LLC, New York

First published in the United States of America by G. P. Putnam's Sons,
an imprint of Penguin Random House LLC, 2022

G. P. Putnam's Sons is a registered trademark of Penguin Random House LLC.

Visit us online at penguinrandomhouse.com

Library of Congress Cataloging-in-Publication Data
Names: Barrows, Annie, author. | Ricks, Sam, illustrator.
Title: Iggy the legend / Annie Barrows; illustrated by Sam Ricks.
Description: New York: G. P. Putnam's Sons, [2022] | Series: Iggy; book 4
Summary: "When Iggy needs to make a bit of money, he conjures up a
scheme to help kids con the Tooth Fairy for profit"—Provided by publisher.
Identifiers: LCCN 2021027950 (print) | 2021027951 (ebook)
ISBN 9780593325339 | ISBN 9780593325346 (ebook)
Subjects: CYAC: Moneymaking projects—Fiction. | Schools—Fiction.
Classification: LCC PZ7.B27576 Ih 2022 (print) | LCC PZ7.B27576 (ebook)
DDC [Fic]—dc23
LC record available at https://lccn.loc.gov/2021027950
LC ebook record available at https://lccn.loc.gov/2021027951

Printed in the United States of America

ISBN 9780593325339

1st Printing

LSCC

Design by Cindy De la Cruz and Marikka Tamura

Text set in New Century Schoolbook LT Std.

To Clio, muse of fourth-grader arcana, with special thanks for the beans in chocolate milk and the horrible yet inspiring story about teeth

—A.B.

To Dr. Ricks, dentist extraordinaire.
To my knowledge, he never lost a tooth in transit,
though he extracted several of mine.

—S.R.

CONTENTS

CHAPTER 1

THINGS TO THINK ABOUT
IF YOU GET HIT OVER THE HEAD
WITH A SHOVEL

Let's talk about blame. Let's talk about how blaming people for things is often wrong and unfair. For example, sometimes people are blamed for things they did by *mistake*, which is wrong and unfair because everyone makes mistakes. If I happen to hit you over the head with a shovel because I tripped, it's totally different than if I tiptoed up behind you and hit you over the head with a shovel. And then laughed.

Which I would never do.

In this way, we can see that it's wrong and unfair to blame people for things they did by mistake.

But sometimes blame is even more wrong and unfair than that!

Sometimes the person being blamed wouldn't have done the bad thing at all if *other* people hadn't done *other* bad things earlier, things that practically forced the first person to do the thing he is being blamed for.

In this way, we can see that other people, especially other people who started it, should get some of the blame for the bad thing too.

Here is a real-life example to help you understand this important idea: If a person gets blamed for a thing he did, and he only did that thing because he needed money, isn't the person who asked him for money partly to blame?

I didn't ask for money!

said Iggy's friend Diego.

It was a membership fee.

There are lots of people who would call it mean, making your friends pay a membership fee to hang out in your back yard. They would call it mean and stingy and little bit like stealing.

It is *not* like stealing!   yelled Diego.

In this example, we learned how wrong and unfair it is to blame only *one* person when this person's "friend" started it by doing a mean, stingy thing.

Would you like another example? I happen to have one.

Let's talk about older sisters, older sisters who are supposed to help and teach their little brothers, but do mean things that ruin their lives instead.

3

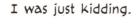

I was just kidding.

said Iggy's sister Maribel.

Oh, great. Just kidding. Just making your little brother suffer so you could have a laugh.

You're not that little!　said Maribel.

Many people would say that if you had helped your little brother when he asked, he wouldn't have needed to do the thing he is being blamed for. "How could anyone be so mean to her little brother?" those people would say. "This sister certainly deserves some of the blame!"

Hey, I'm not the one who—

EXAMPLE NUMBER THREE! How can a person be blamed for breaking a rule that he didn't know was a rule? How is that fair? Did Iggy's parents ever *say* "Oh, by the way, if you ever find something lying on the ground, don't sell it. If you do sell it, you will be a criminal." Many people would say if his parents cared so much about this important rule, they should have mentioned it to him a little earlier.

We shouldn't have to say it!

said Iggy's mom.

You should have known better. You're nine years old!

Iggy is *only* nine years old. He's *only* a kid. He doesn't claim to know everything. How could he? He's a kid. His parents are supposed to teach him the rules. Iggy can only follow the rules if he knows about them.

Ha! said Iggy's dad.

You never follow rules!

What?! Iggy is famous for following rules, if he knows about them! When Monica the lunchroom lady said it was against the rules for Iggy to put his beans in his chocolate milk and call it barf, he stopped. When his teacher, Ms. Schulberger, said he couldn't bring a meat tenderizer to school ever again, he didn't. When his mom told him never to climb out his window onto the roof and bark, he stopped barking! Yes, everyone who knows Iggy* would tell you he is a good kid who follows the rules, if he knows about them.

Now that we have had this interesting conversation about blame, and we've learned that blame is often wrong and unfair, Iggy and I would like to suggest a new way of thinking about the events that occurred between November 16 and November 20, a new and better way that will show that these events, particularly the one everyone's so mad about, are not Iggy's fault. Or not *only* Iggy's fault. We will show that the blame for these events should be shared with many people, including all the ones mentioned above, plus Diego's younger

---

*Except for Mrs. Wander, the principal at Iggy's school; Ms. Dixson, his second-grade teacher; Mr. Sokol, who tried to teach him flute; Rudy Heckie, who lives down the street; Lainey, the nicest girl in the fourth grade; Jeremy Greerson and his mom, who are awfully touchy; Maribel; and assorted other people.

brother, Andrés (the little stinker); a bunch of third graders; the Russian girl; and a forgetful dentist too.

What is our mission? Truth and justice!

Will we free Iggy from the shadow of blame (or at least spread it around a little?), or will Iggy prove to be guilty, guilty, guilty? Only *you* can decide. But you can't decide until after our search for truth and justice is finished, so let's get cracking:

Our story begins back in the old days, the good old days before anyone was mean or stingy or unfair . . .

CHAPTER 2

THE GOOD OLD DAYS OF NOVEMBER 16

Iggy and Diego have been buddies ever since the second day of kindergarten. Iggy has a bunch of other friends, but he probably likes Diego the most.

Why?

What do you mean, *why*?

He just does.

Diego is a really fast runner. Oh, and here's another reason! One day in third grade, Iggy and Diego were in Diego's kitchen, doing homework, and Iggy read his math problem out loud: "6 x E = 24."

"EEEEEEE!" said Diego.

And then they both laughed so hard that milk came out their noses.

That was great.

However, despite being (probably) Iggy's best friend, Diego isn't perfect. Not even close. In fact, sometimes he's a pain in the yonker. As this book will show.

Hey! said Diego.

On November 16, Diego and his dad built a treehouse in Diego's back yard.* Diego and his dad do stuff like that all the time, because Mr. Sandoval (that's Diego's dad) likes to build things, and ever since Diego's little brother, Andrés, broke his own nose with a hammer, Mr. Sandoval usually builds them with Diego. One time they made a go-kart that won second place in a go-kart race.

Iggy's dad doesn't build anything.

I do too!

said Iggy's dad.

I built a bookcase!

---

*Actually, they had started it the weekend before, but that's the kind of detail you get to ignore when you're writing a book.

Big whoop.

Anyway, on November 16, Mr. Sandoval and Diego built a treehouse in Diego's back yard. Pay attention here: On November 16, that's all it was—a treehouse.

But it was an awesome treehouse. It had two parts. It had a part on the ground, under a big tree (there were a lot of trees in Diego's yard), and then a ladder that came out the roof and went up the tree trunk to the other part, the treehouse part. The part on the ground was like a real house, with walls and a window and this cool door that was two half-doors, one on top and one on the bottom. There was a ladder leading to a trapdoor in the roof, and when it opened, you climbed a second ladder on the tree trunk to get to the treehouse part. In the treehouse part, the walls were like balcony walls, so you could look out, but it had a roof. Also a hammock and a bench.

As soon as it was finished, Diego called Iggy. "You gotta come see what my dad and I built," he said. "It's awesome."

And Iggy, a good friend, stopped what he

was doing—which was nothing, but still—and instantly skateboarded three blocks to Diego's house.

Diego and Andrés were standing on the sidewalk in front of their house when he got there. "Hurry up!" yelled Diego when he saw Iggy. "You're going to freak!"

"Yeah, you're going to freak!" said Andrés, jumping up and down.

"Shut up," Diego told Andrés. "Go away."

"Mom said it's my treehouse too!" squeaked Andrés.

Diego rolled his eyes at Iggy in a way that meant, Don't worry; I will soon solve this problem. "Come on!" he said. They zipped around the side of Diego's house and through the gate. Then they zipped through twhe back yard, which was way bigger than Iggy's and had a whole farm section, with spinach and chickens, until they got to the tree section, and Diego said, "Look!"

"Yeah!" said Andrés. "Look!"

Iggy looked, and when he looked, he thought:

Diego's life is better than mine.

He also thought: I want this.
He was jealous.

However, Iggy, a good friend, didn't say these jealous things. He said, *"Sick!"*

Then Iggy and Diego and Andrés crawled through the bottom half-door and swarmed up the ladder to the treehouse and swung in the hammock and threw stuff at squirrels. When they got tired of that, Diego told Andrés to go into the house and bring them some chips. Andrés did. Then Diego told Andrés to go into the house and bring them some dip. Andrés did. Then Diego told Andrés to go into the house and bring them some frosted flakes. Andrés did. And then Iggy and Diego sat on top of the trapdoor so Andrés couldn't get back in.

He yelled for a while, but eventually he went away.

Problem solved.

Up in the treehouse, Diego lay in the hammock with his hands behind his head—Iggy was
stuck with the bench, but he didn't complain—
and said, "I'm going to move all my stuff out and
live here."

Then Iggy reminded him about bath-
rooms, and Diego said he'd pee over the side,
and Iggy said what about the other thing, and
Diego said he'd get a bucket, and Iggy said he'd
get bucket-butt. Then they laughed and threw
more stuff at squirrels, and then Andrés tried

to force his way in, and they threw stuff at him.

Mrs. Sandoval came out on the porch and said Diego should be nice and let Andrés play. Diego said they *were* playing, and she said they were not, but it was time for dinner anyway.

So they climbed down the ladder and crawled through the trapdoor headfirst and crash-landed on Andrés, and Diego went toward his house, yelling over his shoulder, "Bye! Come over tomorrow after school, okay?"

"Yeah!" yelled Iggy over *his* shoulder. "See you tomorrow!"

Yes, everyone was happy and no one was to blame, back in the good old days of November 16.

CHAPTER 3

DIEGO HITS IGGY WITH A CLUB

Remember in the last chapter when I told you that Iggy and Diego have been friends since kindergarten?

Well, I did.

After that year, the school coincidentally made a rule that Iggy and Diego could never be in the same class again.

So Iggy didn't see Diego the next morning (otherwise known as November 17). That morning, he arrived at Ms. Schulberger's room and hissed at the class snake until Ms. Schulberger told him to stop.

Then he pretended to trip over Sarah's feet (they were big) until Ms. Schulberger told him to stop.

Then he tried to balance his book on the tip of his finger until Ms. Schulberger told him to stop.

Then it was Weekend Reports.

If it had been Iggy's turn to give a Weekend Report, he would have told about Diego's treehouse, and it would have been cool and interesting. But it was Cecily's turn, so it was boring. She'd bought a henna kit with her allowance and tooth fairy money. She showed the henna kit. All the girls went "Oooooh!" Iggy pretended to fall asleep until Ms. Schulberger told him to stop.

In other words, a totally normal morning.

Fast-forward to lunch.

In the lunchroom, Iggy sat down next to Diego. But because it's really hard to pay attention when you're hungry, Iggy didn't listen to what Diego was saying until after he'd yammed down two pieces of pizza, one grape, one-half of a carrot stick, and a thing of chocolate milk. Usually, Iggy and Diego ate as fast as they could, wadded up their napkins and threw them at the trash can, returned their trays, and tore out of the lunchroom like maniacs so they'd be at the sports shed in time to get a ball.

Today was no different: When Iggy was done eating, which was about four minutes after he started, he crumpled his pizza paper and napkin into a lump and threw it at the trash can. Basket! "Three points!" he yelled, and turned to get a high five from Diego.

This was when he noticed that Diego wasn't eating. Diego was talking. He was leaning across the table, talking in a low voice to Arch and Aidan and Owen and a kid named Miles Iggy hardly knew.

". . . and sometimes, there'll be overnights, like, we'll sleep up there, except we probably won't sleep that much. No one'll know what we're doing. We can put food in a cooler and have midnight feasts, and I already checked and the internet works out there, so we can play games and watch movies all night if we want—"

Oh, Iggy realized, he's telling them about the treehouse. "It's hecka cool," he reported, because he, Diego's best friend, had been there.

"Sounds hecka cool," muttered Aidan. "How much did you say?"

"Eleven dollars and sixty cents," said Diego. "*Only* eleven sixty."

"Eleven sixty?" asked Iggy. "For what?"

"The membership fee," said Arch.

"The what?" said Iggy.

"To join the *club*," said Miles. "You have to pay eleven sixty to be in it."

"What club?" asked Iggy.

Arch and Aidan and Owen and Miles and even Diego looked at Iggy like he was a slug. Finally, Diego said, "The club we're having in my clubhouse."

"It's a clubhouse?" asked Iggy.

Boy, a lot can happen in four minutes! While Iggy had been yamming pizza, Diego's treehouse had turned into a clubhouse. This meant it was the headquarters of a club.

Guess what kind of club it was.

A video-gaming club?

Nope.

A camping-out club?

Nope.

A let's-keep-our-neighborhood-clean club?

AHAHAHAHA! You're killing me! No.

It was a crime-fighting club.

Why, you ask?

Because it was Diego's club, that's why. He said it was his club and he was the president of it and he could call it whatever he wanted. What he wanted to call it was the Fighting Legends.

He said it sounded awesome in Spanish.* Then
Owen said he wasn't going to be in it because he
didn't want to fight anyone. Diego said
he didn't have to fight anyone.

"Why is it called the Fighting Legends if it's
not about fighting?" asked Owen.

Diego thought for a while, and then he said,
"Because it's a crime-fighting club."

After that, there was a long argument about
which crimes they were going to fight, and it
turned out that all the crimes they could think
of were too dangerous for them to fight, except
possibly cat stealing. They decided that the

---

*Diego was right. In Spanish, it's los Luchadores
Legendarios. Way cooler than English!

main point of the club would be to call the cops if they saw a crime happening (unless someone was stealing a cat, which they would deal with themselves).

By this time, lunch was almost over, and they hadn't even left the table. "What's the holdup?" yelled Monica. (Remember? She's the lunchroom lady.) "Finish your lunch, kids!"

A holdup? They started laughing. "Don't worry, Monica!" Arch yelled. "The Fighting Legends are here!"

Then they ran around, pretending to fight each other until Monica told them to get lost, and they swarmed out the door for the blacktop. Everyone was laughing and goofing around, everyone but Diego. Diego was serious, because he was the club president (even though nobody had elected him), and over the laughing, Diego yelled, "You're not a Fighting Legend until you pay me eleven dollars and sixty cents!"

CHAPTER 4

ONE IS SILVER
AND THE OTHER'S GOLD

Iggy caught up to Diego on the blacktop. "But not me, right?"

"Not you what?" said Diego.

"I don't have to pay eleven sixty to be in the club. Right?"

"Why wouldn't you? Everyone has to pay," said Diego.

Iggy's mouth dropped open. "I'm your best friend!" he yelped.

"Still. You gotta pay," Diego insisted. "It wouldn't be fair if everyone else paid and you didn't. The only person who doesn't have to pay is me. And Andrés," he added glumly. "My mom said I had to let him in."

"I don't have eleven sixty," moaned Iggy.

Diego shrugged.

"You know. I had to buy that lipstick for my mom."*

Diego shrugged again.

"Why are you even charging anything?" demanded Iggy. "Why isn't it free?"

Diego rolled his eyes. "I *said* why: if everyone pays eleven sixty, I can get a *Realms* master edition and we'll all be able to play at once. It isn't that much," he added. "Don't you have any money saved? Didn't you get money for your birthday?"

Iggy didn't say anything. He *had* gotten money for his birthday.

———————

*A terrible story you can read in *The Best of Iggy*, pages 59–73.

On his birthday, he'd been rich. The day after his birthday, he was still rich. Then, the day after that, he'd gone to a place called Laff-Mart and spent twenty-four dollars on rubber waffles and snake-in-a-can and fart spray.

And *then*— Never mind. None of your beeswax.

It was none of Diego's beeswax either.

Iggy noticed an important fact. "Hey! You let me into the treehouse yesterday! I've already been there—for free! It already happened. So I'm already in it."

Diego shook his head. "Doesn't count. That was before it was a club. Now it's a club, so you gotta pay the membership fee. Eleven dollars and sixty cents," he added, in case Iggy had forgotten.

Iggy squinched his eyes into tiny slits. He could say Forget it. He could say I don't want to be in your club anyway. He could say The Fighting Legends is a stupid name and I wouldn't be in it even if it were free. He could say I already went to the clubhouse, and it wasn't that fun. He could even say My real best friend is my cousin Ike.

Unfortunately, none of these things was true.

Iggy *wanted* to be in the club. He thought the Fighting Legends was a cool name for a club. He thought the clubhouse—especially the trapdoor—was awesome. He didn't have a cousin named Ike.

So Iggy unsquinched his eyes and said, "Okay, I'll try to get eleven sixty somehow."

"Cool," said Diego. "When you have it, come over."

CHAPTER 4½

BLAME REASSIGNMENT REPORT #1

I think we can all agree that our search for truth and justice has revealed an important fact: Diego, by demanding his pal Iggy pay him $11.60, caused Iggy to need money, which, as you will see, caused Iggy to do several other things. From this we learn that Diego is at least partly to blame for the events of November 16 to 20, which in turn means Iggy should NOT be blamed anywhere near as much as he is being blamed for those events.

Yay for truth and justice!

CHAPTER 5

IGGY LOOKS FOR WORK

Arch had $11.60.

It was in his closet. He had to go home after school to get it, and then his mom would take him over to Diego's. Then Arch would be a Fighting Legend.

Owen had $11.60 too. He had something to do after school, but the next day, he also would be a Fighting Legend.

Miles and Aidan were going to ask their parents to give them their allowances early. It would be no big deal, they said. They would be Fighting Legends tomorrow too.

Hm.

No big deal.

Iggy decided it was worth a try.

When he got home from school, he practiced in his room. Hi, Mom, can I have some money? Hey, Mom, can I have my allowance early? Mom, no big deal, but I need $11.60.

Okay. It was no big deal. He walked down the hall and opened the door to his mom's workroom. "Hey, Mom, can I have my allowance early?"

His mom looked up from her computer. "Excuse me?"

Iggy smiled a no-big-deal smile. "I really need some money, so I was, um, hoping I could, well, you know—have my allowance early."

His mom's face was not good.

"Please," he added quickly.

"Did you or did you not put fart spray on your sister's comforter?" his mom began.

Oops.

We'll just skip this part.

. . .

. . .

. . .

Okay! Whew! That's done! It is now fifteen minutes later.*

Iggy still didn't have any money, though.

He stood in the hall for a few minutes, thinking. Then he went to the family room and stared at Maribel until she looked up from her homework.

"What?" she said.

"I was just wondering if I could help you with anything?" Iggy remembered to smile.

 "What?"

"Do you need help with anything?" His face felt stretched.

Maribel's eyes got narrow. "What do you want?"

---

*By the way, you don't see Iggy and me trying to say that he's not to blame for this event (which we're not going to discuss), do you? That's how truthful and just *we* are.

"Eleven dollars and sixty cents," said Iggy truthfully.

"Eleven dollars and sixty cents," repeated Maribel. She thought for a moment. Then she smiled. "No problem. I can give you eleven sixty."

"You can?" asked Iggy. "You will?"

Bigger and bigger, Maribel smiled. "Sure. But you have to do everything I tell you for the next three days."

"Oh, right." Iggy rolled his eyes. "You'll tell me to jump off the roof or go lie down in the middle of the street. I'm not an idiot, you know."

Maribel shook her head. "No, I swear! I promise." She held up her right hand. "I won't tell you to do anything that hurts. Only nice, easy things."

"Only nice, easy things?"

"Completely nice, easy things," she confirmed. "Cross my heart."

Iggy thought about it. She had sworn and promised. She had crossed her heart. "Okay," he said. "Give me eleven sixty, and I'll do something nice and easy."

Maribel began to giggle. "Good," she said. "My money's upstairs."

CHAPTER 6

LYING DOWN
IN THE MIDDLE OF THE STREET
BEGINS TO SOUND PRETTY GOOD

Upstairs, Maribel laid one five-dollar bill, five one-dollar bills, and six quarters on her desk. She started to put down a dime too, but Iggy (Fairly! Honestly!) said, "That's okay. I have a dime." He crumpled the money into a ball and jammed it into a sock. Then he turned to Maribel. "What do I have to do?"

Maribel had that smile again. "First, you get on your knees and say, 'You are the most awesome sister in the history of the world. You are also a genius and beautiful.'"

Iggy made a face. "Ew. Get out of here. No."

"Excuse me?" It was amazing how much she sounded like Iggy's mom.

Iggy thought about the Fighting Legends. Midnight feasts. Video games. The trapdoor. He got down on his knees. "Youarethemostawesome-sisterinthehistoryoftheworldyouarealsoagenius-andpretty."

"Beautiful," she corrected.

"Beautiful," he muttered.

"Say the whole thing again," she ordered.

"Aw, come on!" Iggy whined. His knees hurt.

"Excuse me?" said Maribel.

"Youarethemostawesomesisterinthehistory-oftheworldyouarealsoageniusand-beautiful." He almost gagged.

Maribel nodded. "Good."

Iggy staggered to his feet, muttering things about nice and easy. "Okay," he said. "Thanks for the money." He turned to go to his room.

"Excuse me?" There she went again! "Get back here. That was just the beginning. For the next part, you'll need a glue stick."

• • •

By eight o'clock that night, Iggy had glued Maribel's diorama of Canadian fur traders (and his fingers too); he had typed her language arts paragraph (which took a long time, because of his fingers being gluey); he had set the table for her; and then he had set the table for her again because she didn't like the way he'd folded the napkins; he had brought her milk; he had brought her ice cream; he had carried her plate into the kitchen; and he had cleared off the table.

"It's so nice of you to help Maribel with her chores!" his mom said, beaming.

"Hunh," grunted Iggy. All the real words he was thinking would have gotten him in trouble.

"Okay, Ig," said Maribel sweetly. "Let's go."

"No way!" he protested. "I already did everything! There's nothing left to do!"

Maribel laughed. "That's what you think. It's time for my pedicure!"

• • •

"Don't breathe on my feet," Maribel said.

"What? I'm supposed to not breathe? I have to breathe!" said Iggy. "It's not like I want to breathe your stupid feet anyway."

"Stop talking! It's about to drip!" squawked Maribel.

A bright drop of purple nail polish splattered on Iggy's pants. "Oh, man!" he yelped. "Look what you made me do!"

"I did not! It's you!" snapped Maribel. "You're not paying attention!"

"I am too! This is stupid!" shouted Iggy.

"Stop yelling! You're going to drip it again!"

"I'm not going to drip—"

"Ahhh! You dripped! You ruined it! Ew! It's on my toe, you big doofus!" Maribel flicked Iggy on the head. "Now you have to start all over again."

"It's fine!" bellowed Iggy. "It looks gross anyway! I'm not doing it again!"

"Oh yes, you are!"

"Oh no, I'm not!"

"You have to fix it!" She flicked his head again.

"No I don't," said Iggy. "I quit." He turned the bottle of nail polish upside down over Maribel's toes, and very shortly after that, Iggy became, once again, a person who didn't have $11.60.

CHAPTER 6½

BLAME REASSIGNMENT REPORT #2

Our search for truth and justice—which is going really well, in our opinion—clearly shows that Maribel, who could have helped Iggy and didn't, who oppressed and tormented him instead, is partly to blame for the events that occurred between November 16 and November 20, which in turn means—what?

Sheesh! Pay attention!

It means that Iggy should not be blamed anywhere near as much as he is being blamed for those events.

CHAPTER 7

THE MANDIBLES OF FATE

The next morning (November 18), Iggy dragged himself sadly to school. He slomped sadly into Ms. Schulberger's classroom. He was too sad to trip over Sarah's feet or hiss at the class snake. When Cecily showed her henna tattoos and all the girls went "Oooooh!" Iggy didn't say they looked like chicken footprints (which they did). That's how sad he was. He just sat there while Ms. Schulberger talked about the difference between regular writing and a poem, and he didn't bother to groan when she said they each had to write a poem. He just did it, that's how sad he was. Ms. Schulberger said it

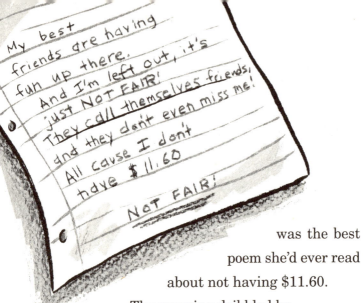

My best
friends are having
fun up there.
And I'm left out, it's
just NOT FAIR!
They call themselves friends,
and they don't even miss me!
All cause I don't
have $11.60

NOT FAIR!

was the best
poem she'd ever read
about not having $11.60.

The morning dribbled by.

Then it was lunch.

Guess what Diego and Arch and Aidan and Owen and Miles talked about excitedly in the lunchroom.

Right.

Iggy was too sad to eat. Except for three tacos and a grape.

After school, the Fighting Legends went to Diego's house for their first meeting.

Iggy slomped home.

• • •

There are some people who say that going into nature is the key to happiness. If you're in a

bad mood, these people will say "Go outside, breathe the fresh air, look at the trees, listen to the birdies, and you will be happy."

Guess what!

These people are big liars.

The truth is, nature is out to get you.

At least, it was out to get Iggy.

Sometime during the afternoon of November 18, Iggy was ordered outside. Specifically, he was ordered to walk around the block and see if he could come back in a better mood.

"I know when I'm not wanted!" he hollered as he left. He may have slammed the door. He stomped down the front path, down the front stairs, down the block. Did he see the little birdies and the big trees and feel joy? No. He saw the same old regular boring things he had already seen a million times and felt crabby. House, flowers. Fence, apartment house, flowers, trees. He went down another block. Houses, bushes, trees, houses, bushes, trees. Still crabby! What was the matter with being crabby,

anyway? He crossed the street and went down another block. Houses, rocks, trees—

Wait.

Iggy stopped in his tracks.

It couldn't be.

Iggy looked again.

It was.

Picture this: Iggy was standing on a sidewalk. On one side of him, there was a house, just a regular house, with a regular yard, with all the regular bushes and flowers. On the other side of him, there was that grassy space—you know, that space that has no name—between the sidewalk and the curb. In this grassy, no-name space beside Iggy, there was a tree. And in the grass, among the roots of the tree, there was a bag of teeth.

No way.

Teeth?

Iggy leaned over to take a closer look.

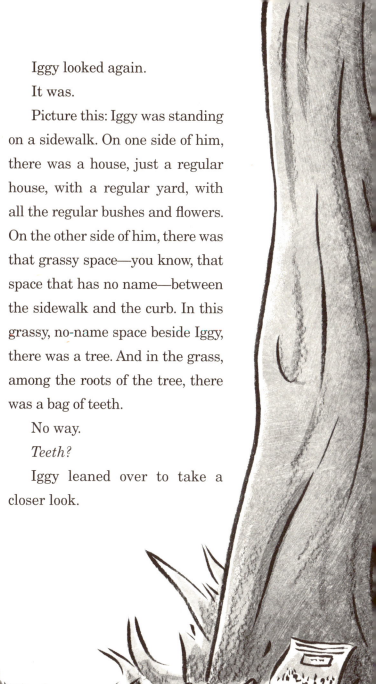

It was teeth. Inside a bag, the kind with a zipper top, there were hundreds of shiny little whitish teeth.

Iggy poked the bag with his foot. It didn't explode.

Iggy looked around to see if anyone was watching. No one was watching.

He picked up the bag. It felt sort of like a beanbag. Except with teeth.

Iggy looked up and down the sidewalk. Did the teeth belong to someone? No one was running toward him, screaming "My teeth! My teeth! I lost my teeth!"

Just to be sure, Iggy turned the bag over to see if there was a name on it. There was a label, but on the label it said MAND. PREM. #2, which obviously wasn't anyone's name. No one is named Mand. Prem. #2.

Finders keepers.

That was the rule. Even grown-ups said so. Even grown-ups said that if you were walking along and you saw a quarter, you could pick it up and keep it. It wasn't stealing; it was finding. Iggy had always wanted to find a puppy. Instead, he had found teeth.

Iggy opened the bag and looked at the teeth. They were perfectly clean. They were all the same color. They weren't bloody. They weren't cracked. They didn't have cavities.

They were probably fake, Iggy decided.

But they looked real.

Anyone would think they were real. Especially a grown-up. Especially a grown-up mom or dad whose kid said "Lookit, I lost my tooth."

Iggy's own teeth started to show because he was smiling. If someone had given him the choice between finding a puppy and finding a bag of teeth, he'd have chosen the puppy. But now that he'd found a bag of teeth, he was happy. You can't take a puppy to school and sell it.

CHAPTER 7½

BLAME REASSIGNMENT REPORT #3

What do we discover here, friends? We discover that Iggy was sent out of his house by his mom. Did she say, before he left, "Oh, Iggy, if you find a bag of something, don't pick it up, okay?" No, she did not, and she had never said it before either. As far as he knew, *finders keepers* was the rule unless it was obviously something that had been lost by someone. The bag of teeth had no name on it; it was not obviously anyone's. I think we can all agree that as far as he knew, Iggy was breaking NO rules when he picked up his bag of teeth.

Keep this in mind when you get to chapter thirteen.

CHAPTER 8

TRUTH IN ADVERTISING, AT LEAST

You know how sometimes you buy something and it doesn't work? For example, you buy a rubber waffle, and on the package it says *Fool Your Friends! Looks Just Like Real!* There's even a picture on the package of an amazed kid with a rubber waffle hanging out of his mouth, and around him, a circle of kids doubled over with laughter. Some of them are laughing so hard that tears are flying off their faces, that's how funny it's supposed to be.

But then, let's say you can't wait for a friend to turn up, so you try it on your little sister, Molly, because she's only three and pretty easy to fool, and it turns out totally different than the package. Molly doesn't even try to eat the waffle; she just licks the syrup off the rubber. Plus, nobody thinks it's funny. In fact, everyone is mad because Molly and the kitchen are sticky.

The package promised big laughs, but nobody laughed at all.

This is called false advertising.

It's actually a crime.

The person who made the package is supposed to get in big trouble.

Guess who got in trouble instead?

Right!

Iggy.

If we started to talk about unfair blame in this incident, we'd never stop. So we're going to talk about how honest Iggy is. How honest and upstanding and good.

You see, after the kitchen portion of the rubber-waffle incident was over, and Iggy was in the go-to-your-room-and-think-about-what-you've-done portion, he said to himself—thinking about what had been done to him— that *he* would never sell something that didn't work; *he* would never lie on a package; *he* would never commit the crime of false advertising and ruin the lives of his customers.

Now, holding a bag of teeth, did Iggy forget these vows?

No!

Iggy remembered the misery and suffering that could be caused by false advertising, and he did the honest thing. The right thing. The good thing.

He tried it himself to make sure it worked.

• • •

After dinner, Iggy went to his room and took a single tooth from the bag. He spat on it. Then, holding it in his hand, he went downstairs, where his mom and dad were talking about coffee, and said, "Hey! I lost a tooth!" He held out the tooth for them to see.

The usual thing happened: His dad glanced at it and said, "Wow, that's a good one." And his mom smiled and talked about how cute he was when he didn't have any teeth.

(Speaking of lies.)

Then Iggy said, just a little louder than normal, "I'll put it under my pillow tonight!"

His mom and dad nodded and went back to talking about coffee.

"Gosh, I hope the tooth fairy gives me a dollar fifty for this one," said Iggy, very loudly.

"The tooth fairy is not made of money," said his dad.

Iggy left the room.

Fast-forward two hours: Time for bed. Iggy put the tooth under his pillow.

It worked. The next morning (that's November 19, people), Iggy was one dollar richer, and he had a product he could guarantee. He put the dollar and his dime into his sock. $10.50 to go.

CHAPTER 9

BUCK TEETH

One of the most surprising things Iggy discovered from his bag of teeth was this: Third graders are amazingly rich.

Another thing he learned: They aren't so good at subtraction.

At morning recess, over on the third-grader part of the playground, Iggy explained it: You pay a quarter for a tooth; you get a dollar from the tooth fairy; you have made 75 cents.

"What?" said the third graders.

He explained it again.

"What?" said the third graders.

He was just about to start yelling at them when a kid named Serena said, "Oh! I get it." She explained it in some sort of special third-grader language.

"Ohhhh!" cried the third graders. Then they started yanking quarters out of their pockets. Iggy couldn't believe it. Why did they have so much money? Didn't they know how to buy stuff? It was like they had been saving up for teeth.

By lunch recess, Iggy was surrounded by third graders, and even some second graders, desperate to buy teeth.

"Give me four!" said a kid named Antonio.

"That'll be one dollar," said Iggy. "At the special introductory price of a quarter each."

He liked to say this as often as possible.

Antonio pulled four quarters out of his pocket as if it were nothing.

Amazing. Iggy took four Mand. Prem. #2s from his stash and dropped them into Antonio's palm. "Don't use them all at once," he warned.

"Why not?" said Antonio. "I'll get four dollars."

"Yeah, but you'll get caught too," said Iggy

wisely. "Nobody loses four teeth at the same time. Your parents will notice you don't have four teeth missing."

Antonio thought about it. "They don't notice much. They just had twins."

"Listen, kid, I'm a pro," said Iggy. "Try two now and save two for later."

Antonio looked down at the teeth. "Maybe you're right. I could keep two for when I really need money."

"Right!" said Iggy. "It's like money in the bank."

"Hurry up!" yelled the kids in line.

● ● ●

After school, Diego and Arch and Owen and Aidan and Miles took off for the clubhouse, but Iggy didn't mind. Yesterday, he had been down and out, but today, Iggy was a successful businessman! He walked home, his backpack jingling with seventeen quarters. Otherwise known as $4.25. For sure, he still needed $6.25, but he had orders for twelve teeth from kids who were bringing money tomorrow, which meant—Iggy sat down on the curb to do the math—a total of

$3.00. Which, added to the seventeen quarters he'd made that day and the dollar from his own tooth the night before, gave him a grand total of—Iggy squeezed his head to do the math—$8.25!* Which meant—Iggy hit himself on the head to do the math—he still needed $3.25.

"Why are you hitting your head?" asked a voice above him.

It was the Russian girl. She was famous. "I'm doing math," explained Iggy. "In my head."

She frowned. "Math is better without hitting."

Iggy shrugged. To each their own.

"You have teeth?" she asked. "To sell?"

Iggy nodded.

"I want thirteen."

"You want thirteen?" asked Iggy.

She nodded.

"It's not going to work," Iggy told her.

"Yes, please. Thirteen," she repeated. "Three and ten."

"You're in fifth grade," Iggy tried to explain.

---

*Yeah, yeah, I know, he wasn't including the dime he already had. You add the dime in your head if you're so great.

70

"You already lost most of your teeth. No one will believe you."

She frowned. "Believe me?"

"No one will believe they fell out. No one will give you money."

"Who gives money?"

"The tooth fairy!" yelled Iggy.

The Russian girl looked at him like he was crazy. "A fairy with teeth?"

"No! The tooth fairy brings you money when your teeth fall out!"

She hesitated. "Nice story for nice boy. I want thirteen." She pulled a pouch from the neck of her shirt. "I have money."

Iggy stared at her.

"It isn't necessary to hit your head," she said. "Three dollars and twenty-five cents."

Exactly what he needed. Still. "What are you going to do with them?" Iggy asked.

"You have change?" she said, handing him a five.

"What are you going to do with them?" he asked again.

"It is one dollar and seventy-five cents," she said helpfully.

"I know." He gave her seven of his quarters. "What are you going to do with them?"

"Now the teeth." She held out her hand. "Thirteen," she added, in case he'd forgotten. "Three and ten."

Iggy opened his backpack, counted out thirteen Mand. Prems., and gave them to her. "What are you going to do with them?" he asked very slowly.

She smiled. "Don't worry, nice boy. Thank you for teeth." Pause. "The teeth," she corrected herself.

Iggy tried a different way. "What do kids in Russia do with their teeth when they fall out?"

"They give them to rats," she said.*

*I'm not making this up. Look it up if you don't believe me.

CHAPTER 10

THE FIGHTING LEGENDS

At 3:05 p.m. on November 20, Iggy received his final quarter. He had $11.60! But not on him (quarters are heavy). He tore home, gathered all his money, plus the leftover teeth (because you never knew when you might make a sale), and raced toward Diego's house to become—at last!—a Fighting Legend.

When he arrived, panting and jingling, the other Legends (except Aidan, who had rugby)

were already in the treehouse, sitting on the bench in a row. Diego reclined on the hammock. "Put the money over there," he directed Iggy, pointing to a corner.

Iggy poured twenty-two quarters and one dime onto the floor and laid the five and the one on top. "Ta-DA!" he said proudly, gesturing at his pile.

"You want me to count it, Diego?" squeaked Andrés. "I can count it."

"No," said Diego. "Nobody wants you to do anything."

"What's *he* doing here?" asked Iggy.

"I told you. My mom made me."

"So I'm in?" asked Iggy.

Diego nodded. "Yup. You're in."

"Yeah!" yelled Iggy.

Arch and Owen and Miles didn't say anything.

"So? That's it?" Iggy asked. He a little disappointed. He didn't know what he had expected. A cheer, maybe? A party? Whatever it was, he wasn't getting it.

"That's it," muttered Arch.

Iggy glanced around the treehouse. The Fighting Legends did not look as happy as he had imagined them being. They didn't look like they were having the most fun ever. They didn't look like they'd recently been laughing their heads off. Actually, they looked a little bored. "Okay!" said Iggy, hoping they would pep up. "What do we do now? Video games? Even if you don't have *Realms* yet, we could still play *Tracker Z*, right?"

Arch and Owen and Miles looked at Diego. Diego looked at the floor. "No video games," said Owen. "We used up too much data on Tuesday."

"Dad got mad!" said Andrés. "Dad said they were a bunch of—"

"Shut up," groaned Diego.

No video games? "Bummer," said Iggy. What else was there? It was of course not midnight, so no midnight feasts. But—"What about snacks?" asked Iggy.

Arch and Owen and Diego looked at Miles. Miles looked at the floor. "Miles drank all Mom's oil!" reported Andrés. "So they can't go in the kitchen anymore."

"You drank *oil*?" Iggy asked Miles.

"I like oil," said Miles. "Okay?"

"It was Mom's fancy truffle oil," squeaked Andrés.

"She only uses it at Christmas and it costs twenty-nine dollars and Diego had to buy more!"

Iggy winced sympathetically. "Ooh, that's worse than lipstick."

"And then these guys said I had to buy them snacks," Diego said.

"Great!" said Iggy. "Let's eat!"

"They already ate them. They ate everything in, like, two and a half minutes," said Diego. "I didn't get any. Even though *I* bought them."

"With our money," said Arch, like he'd said it before. "Our membership fee."

"Still," said Diego, like he'd said it before.

Diego's broke!

Andrés said.

"Shut up!" Diego groaned.

"So . . . what have you guys been doing?" asked Iggy, even though he thought he knew the answer.

"We don't do anything," said Miles, making a face at Diego.

"Hey, I showed you that card trick," said Diego.

Nobody said anything. Iggy thought it probably hadn't been a very good card trick. "Any crime fighting?" he asked hopefully.

"Pffft," said Arch, which meant No.

Iggy began to feel a little bit cheated. "I just paid eleven dollars and sixty cents to sit around? I can sit around for *free*!"

"Yeah," said Miles. "I'm not getting any allowance for three weeks, and all we do is sit around."

"I was going to buy a pack of those huge Sharpies," said Owen. "And now I can't."

"No refunds," said Diego.

"Yeah! No refunds!" squalled Andrés. "He's broke!"

Iggy looked at his quarters. "I had to sell *teeth* to make that money," he said.

Everyone turned to look at him.

"Open your mouth," said Diego.

"Not *my* teeth, you dweeb!" said Iggy. He pulled his bag of Mand. Prem. #2s from his backpack and showed the Legends. "Didn't you guys wonder where I was for the past two days? I was selling teeth!"

All ten of their eyebrows went up. They hadn't wondered. They didn't say anything for a moment. Finally Arch asked, "Where'd you get those teeth?"

"I found them," said Iggy.

"You found a bag of *teeth*?" said Miles.

"Yeah," said Iggy. "And then I sold them."

"Sold them to who? Why would anyone buy teeth?" asked Diego, looking confused.

"To kids! Duh! So they could say their teeth had fallen out and get tooth fairy money." Iggy looked around at his friends. What didn't they get? "I charged them a quarter."

"Wait," said Arch. But he didn't say anything afterward.

They were like the third graders; Iggy had to explain. "Most kids get a dollar when they lose a tooth, right? So if they pay me a quarter, they still make seventy-five cents."

Arch whistled in admiration.

"That's genius," said Miles. "You thought it up?"

Iggy nodded. Now that he was telling them about it, he noticed that it was, actually, genius.

"And you just *found* the bag?" asked Miles.

Iggy nodded. He was pretty lucky, he noticed. Not many people found a bag of teeth.

"How many do you have left?" asked Owen, looking at the bag enviously.

Iggy shrugged. "A hundred, maybe? I didn't count them."

Whoa.

Cool.

That's, wait—that's twenty-five dollars.

Wow.

"It was actually pretty fun, selling them," Iggy said, remembering the good times. "The Russian girl bought thirteen."

"Dude," said Arch. "You *talked* to the Russian girl?"

Iggy nodded modestly. He knew what he saw. His friends thought selling teeth was cool. They thought *he* was cool for thinking of it. They wished *they* had thought of it. They wished *they* had found a bag of teeth. They wished *they* had talked to the Russian girl. They wished *they* had as much money (in teeth) as he did. They wished they were him.

"You're lucky," said Miles. "We spent all that money, and we just sit around doing nothing."

"Oh, come on," began Diego. "We *will* do stuff. We'll do . . ." His voice trailed off. "Lots of stuff."

"Like what? We can't play video games, and we don't have snacks," said Owen gloomily. "What else is there?"

"And it's not like there are any crimes," sighed Arch.

"Wish there were," sighed Miles.

Suddenly, there was a squeaking sound. It was coming from Andrés. He jumped up.

"There is too!" he cried. "There is too a crime!" He pointed at Iggy. "That thing he's doing? With the tooth fairy? It's lying. It's a crime." He looked proudly around the treehouse. "I'm going to call the police!"

He started for the ladder.

CHAPTER 11

THE NEXT FOUR MINUTES

The next four minutes were fun.

The Fighting Legends, who only a moment before had felt so unhappy about their club that they were ready to quit, suddenly became full of club spirit. They were the Fighting Legends! They were united! Maybe they weren't exactly united to fight crime, but who cares? They were united to fight little squealer brothers!

Since Owen was sitting closest to the ladder, he tried to grab Andrés as he went by.

Unfortunately, Owen was the slowest of the Fighting Legends, and Andrés got away, screaming, "Hey! Hey! Crime! There's crime up here!"

Andrés fell down the tree-trunk ladder and thumped into the trapdoor, which gave the rest of the Fighting Legends a chance to thunder down after him. But just as Diego—roaring, "Shut up, you little stinker!"—was on the verge of nabbing him, Andrés managed to pull the trapdoor up and scramble down into the lower house and out the little half-door.

Seeing this, Iggy heroically jumped off the roof of the bottom house and began to chase Andrés around the yard. Miles, inspired by

Iggy's heroism, also jumped off the roof and began to chase Andrés. Arch and Diego popped out the lower door and joined the other Fighting Legends in chasing Andrés around the back yard until he tried to crawl under a chicken coop and Diego yanked him out by his ankles.

Andrés screamed, "CRIME, CRIME, CRIME!"

Diego dragged him around, yelling, "Shut *up*, you little poop!"

The chickens, seeing an opportunity, ran for freedom.

The Fighting Legends started chasing the chickens.

The chickens lost their minds.

"CRIME,   CRIME,   CRIME,"
screamed Andrés.

"SQUAWK!" screamed the chickens.

"FIGHTING LEGENDS RULE!"
screamed Iggy and Miles and Arch.

"YAAAAH!" screamed Owen.

ZE!

screamed
Mr. Sandoval.

CHAPTER 12

MINUTE FIVE

The chickens were
still having fun.

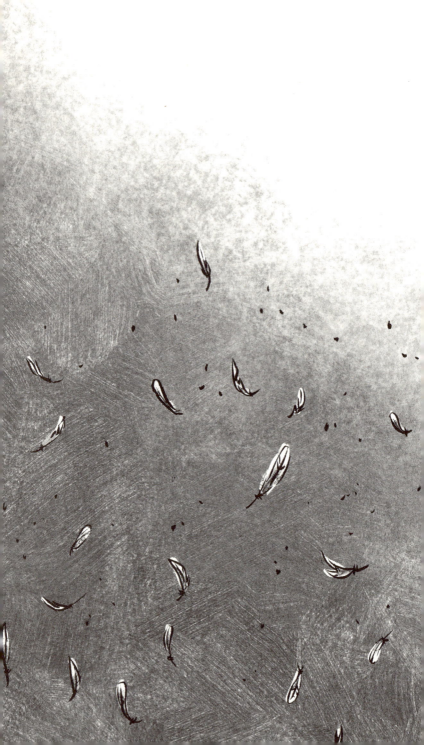

CHAPTER 13

MINUTES SIX THROUGH THREE HUNDRED

We don't really need to discuss this, do we?

We do?

Really?

Okay. Fine.

The period between Minute Six and Minute Three Hundred was when Iggy learned that there were several rules that his parents had forgotten to teach him. And that he was in trouble for breaking them anyway.

Would you like to know what they are, just in case your parents have also forgotten to teach you these rules?

RULES IGGY'S PARENTS
HAD FORGOTTEN TO TEACH HIM
(BUT WERE STILL MAD ABOUT)

1. You're not supposed to pick up stuff
   you find on the street.
   [Even though these are the very same
   people who had taught Iggy the idea
   of *finders keepers*. Would you like to
   know *how* they taught Iggy this? By
   taking a big drawing pad they found
   on the sidewalk home for Molly to
   use. How is this different from a bag
   of teeth? It isn't!]

2. If you do find stuff on the street,
   you're not supposed to sell it.
   [Why not? What was the Gold Rush
   but people finding stuff
   in the dirt and
   selling it?]

3. If the thing you sell is teeth, and the people who buy the teeth use them to cheat their parents, it's as if you cheated their parents yourself.
   [What? That's ridiculous! If the kids who bought Iggy's teeth cheated their parents, how is that his fault? He didn't *make* them lie to their parents, did he? No! It was their own choice, so it was their own crime! He just had an idea. Why is he to blame?]

4. If you get money by lying, it's like you stole it.
   [Wellll, okay. They *had* kind of taught Iggy that idea. I mean, they had *mentioned* that he wasn't supposed to lie . . .]

Still, he himself had only lied about one tooth. And he'd only received one dollar.

He apologized. "Sorry," he said. It seemed like plenty of apologizing for just one dollar.

Apparently, it wasn't.

Because after this came . . .

CHAPTER 14

MINUTES THREE HUNDRED THROUGH TEN THOUSAND AND EIGHTY

Let's just say that if ruining someone's life for a week were a crime, Iggy's parents would be criminals too.

CHAPTER 15

THE SEARCH FOR TRUTH AND JUSTICE BEGINS

A couple of weeks later, Iggy and Diego were waiting in the line outside the sports shed when Diego nudged Iggy in the ribs. "The Russian girl!" he hissed. "She's coming over."

It was true.

"Hello, Ziggy," she said. There was a rumor she was already six feet tall. "Have you more teeth?"

Iggy shook his head. "I don't have them anymore. My parents took them."

"I heard this. I hoped it was not true." She sighed. "It's very bad. I need thirty-two more."

Thirty-two teeth? Very slowly, Iggy asked, "What do you do with them?"

"I make art," she said. "Beautiful art." She opened her jacket so Iggy could see her T-shirt. On it, there was a girl's head. She had long pink hair and a giant mouth with Iggy's teeth glued inside it.

Iggy made a noise that he turned into "Wow!"

"Yes, many people want one like this. I need more teeth."

"I got in a lot of trouble for selling them."

The Russian girl made a face. "But this is unfair. You need money, you find teeth, you sell them to me, I make beautiful art. Where is the wrong in this?"

That was a very good question! Where *was* the wrong?

"If this were a good world, you would have no need of money. This friend"—she glared at Diego, who turned red—"he wouldn't ask you for money. He would be a real friend. He would *give* you money. Why do you get punished? Why not the friend who asked for money?"

"Yeah!" said Iggy, turning around to glare at Diego too.

"And selling teeth," the Russian girl continued. "Why is this bad? Here, everyone sells things. It is almost a rule, you must sell things. Do people say Oh yes, you can sell everything *except* teeth? I don't think so."

"That's true!" said Iggy. "They didn't tell me it was against the rules. They just got mad at me for doing it. Well, also for lying," he admitted.

She shook her head. "Psh, lying! Fairies with teeth? Fairies have no teeth. This is already a lie."

"You know what? You're right," said Iggy. "Grown-ups lie about all sorts of stuff!"

The Russian girl sighed. "And then they blame you," she agreed.

Suddenly, Iggy could see it all: He had been blamed unfairly and wrongly. He had been punished for others' actions. How terrible! Suddenly, in that moment, Iggy knew he must begin a great search for truth and justice.

But also suddenly in that moment, he and Diego reached the front of the line and scored one of the two soccer balls that wasn't wrecked. "Sweet!" Iggy said, grabbing it. "Let's go!"

So the search for truth and justice had to wait for a while.

IN CONCLUSION

BLAME REASSIGNMENT FINAL REPORT

The Blame Reassignment Commission now
concludes its investigation into Iggy
Frangi's blame for the events of November
16 through 20. The Commission has determined that the previous amount of blame
received by Iggy for these events (see
Figure A) was incorrect.

Figure A: Iggy's Blame, Before

The Blame Reassignment Commission has determined that the correct amount of Iggy Frangi's blame for these events is, in fact, as follows (see Figure B).

Figure B: Iggy's Blame, Now

The Blame Reassignment Commission has further determined that the remaining blame must be divided as follows (see Figure C).

Figure C: Corrected Blame for the Events of November 16–20

Diego's Blame	18%
Maribel's Blame	15%
Mom and Dad's Blame	17%
Andrés's Blame (the little stinker)	31%
The Blame of Assorted Third and Second Graders	7%
The Russian Girl's Blame	2%
Iggy's Blame	3%
The Forgetful Dentist's Blame	7%

Please adjust your blame accordingly.

photo credit: Amy Perl Photography

ANNIE BARROWS regrets to report that she is to blame for the following things: dropping the iron on the kitchen floor (twice); microwaving her children's sippy cups (sorry about that, kids); and declaring in print that Komodo dragons don't poop (they do). Everything else she ever did was fine. Even the thing with the Barbie shoes. It wasn't *her* idea.

anniebarrows.com

@anniebarrowsauthor

SAM RICKS is the illustrator of the Geisel Award winner *Don't Throw It to Mo!* and the Stinkbomb and Ketchup-Face books. He is grateful his parents let him live through a surprising number of Iggycidents. Sam lives with his family in Utah.

samricks.com

@samuelricks

DON'T MISS IGGY'S NEXT TRIUMPHS

COMING SOON!

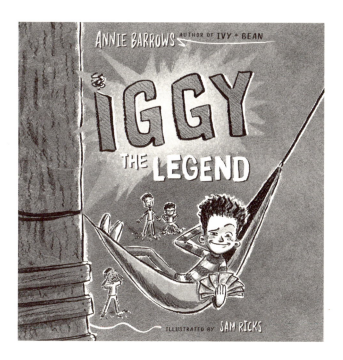